MIDLOTHIAN PUBLIC LIBRARY
3 1614 00141 9820

W9-BIU-779

Fran and Fay Find a Bird

The Sound of F

by Joanne Meier and Cecilia Minden · illustrated by Bob Ostrom

The Child's World

Published by The Child's World®
1980 Lookout Drive
Mankato, MN 56003-1705
800-599-READ
www.childsworld.com

The Child's World®: Mary Berendes, Publishing Director
The Design Lab: Design and page production

Library of Congress Cataloging-in-Publication Data
Meier, Joanne D.
Fran and fay find a bird : the sound of f / by Joanne Meier and Cecilia Minden ; illustrated by Bob Ostrom.
p. cm.
ISBN 978-1-60253-400-1 (library bound : alk. paper)
1. English language–Consonants–Juvenile literature. 2. English language–Phonetics–Juvenile literature 3. Reading–Phonetic method–Juvenile literature. I. Minden, Cecilia. II. Ostrom, Bob. III. Title.
PE1159.M455 2010
[E]–dc22 2010002913

Printed in the United States of America in Mankato, MN.
July 2010
F11538

NOTE TO PARENTS AND EDUCATORS:

The Child's World® has created this series with the goal of exposing children to engaging stories and illustrations that assist in phonics development. The books in the series will help children learn the relationships between the letters of written language and the individual sounds of spoken language. This contact helps children learn to use these relationships to read and write words.

The books in this series follow a similar format. An introductory page, to be read by an adult, introduces the child to the phonics feature, or sound, that will be highlighted in the book. Read this page to the child, stressing the phonic feature. Help the student learn how to form the sound with her mouth. The story and engaging illustrations follow the introduction. At the end of the story, word lists categorize the feature words into their phonic elements.

Each book in this series has been carefully written to meet specific readability requirements. Close attention has been paid to elements such as word count, sentence length, and vocabulary. Readability formulas measure the ease with which the text can be read and understood. Each book in this series has been analyzed using the Spache readability formula.

Reading research suggests that systematic phonics instruction can greatly improve students' word recognition, spelling, and comprehension skills. This series assists in the teaching of phonics by providing students with important opportunities to apply their knowledge of phonics as they read words, sentences, and text.

This is the letter f.

In this book, you will read words that have the **f** sound as in: *fish*, *five*, *food*, and *four*.

This is Fran and Fay.

They are five.

Fran and Fay find a bird.

"Why can't the bird fly?"

asks Fay.

"His wing is hurt," says Fran.

"We can help the bird."

"Let's find a safe place for
the bird to rest," says Fay.

Dr.Flo

"We will take the bird to the doctor. Dr. Flo can fix the bird," says Fran.

Fran and Fay find Dr. Flo.
She is feeding some fish.

"Can you help this bird?" asks Fay.

"I will try. The bird must rest for four days," says Dr. Flo.

"We will give him food and water. We will help him fly."

Fran and Fay look at the bird. "Don't worry, bird! Soon you will fly far away."

Dr.Flo

"This bird is lucky to find
two friends like you!"
says Dr. Flo.

Fun Facts

Some fish can live longer than human beings. Rougheye rockfish are found in the Pacific Ocean. They can live to be more than 200 years old! While most fish live underwater, lungfish are able to survive in mud puddles. Lungfish have been around for more than 300 million years and live in Africa, South America, and Australia.

Most birds use their wings to fly, but certain birds such as penguins and ostriches don't fly at all! Some scientists believe that certain birds can fly at speeds of up to 200 miles (322 kilometers) per hour.

Activity

Fish Watching

If you are interested in fish, take a trip to your local aquarium. You'll probably be able to see many kinds of fish, as well as other interesting water animals. Some aquariums even have special presentations that allow visitors to watch the fish as they are being fed. If you have a fish tank of your own at home, keep a journal. In it, describe what the fish look like, how often you feed them, and how they are different from one another.

To Learn More

Books

About the Sound of F

Moncure, Jane Belk. *My "f" Sound Box®*. Mankato, MN: The Child's World, 2009.

About Fish

Lundblad Kristina, and Bobbie Kalman. *Animals Called Fish*. New York: Crabtree Publishing, 2005.

Pfeffer, Wendy, and Holly Keller (illustrator). *What's It Like to Be a Fish?* New York: HarperCollins, 1996.

About Flying

Anholt, Laurence. *Leonardo and the Flying Boy*. Hauppauge, NY: Barron's Juveniles, 2007.

Glover, David. *Flying and Floating*. New York: Kingfisher Books, 2001.

About Friends

Brown, Laurene Krasny, and Marc Brown. *How to Be a Friend: A Guide to Making Friends and Keeping Them*. Boston: Little, Brown, & Co., 1998.

Carle, Eric, and Kazuo Iwamura. *Where Are You Going? To See My Friend!* New York: Orchard Books, 2003.

Web Sites

Visit our home page for lots of links about the Sound of F:

childsworld.com/links

Note to Parents, Teachers, and Librarians: We routinely check our Web links to make sure they're safe, active sites–so encourage your readers to check them out!

F Feature Words

Proper Names

Fay
Flo
Fran

Feature Words in Initial Position

far
feeding
find
fish
five
fix
fly
food
for
four
friends

Feature Words in Final Position

safe

About the Authors

Joanne Meier, PhD, has worked as an elementary school teacher, university professor, and researcher. She earned her BA in early childhood education from the University of South Carolina, and her MEd and PhD in education from the University of Virginia. She currently works as a literacy consultant for schools and private organizations. Joanne lives in Virginia with her husband Eric, daughters Kella and Erin, two cats, and a gerbil.

Cecilia Minden, PhD, is the former director of the Language and Literacy Program at the Harvard Graduate School of Education. She is now a reading consultant for school and library publications. She earned her PhD in reading education from the University of Virginia. Cecilia and her husband, Dave Cupp, live outside Chapel Hill, North Carolina. They enjoy sharing their love of reading with their grandchildren, Chelsea and Qadir.

About the Illustrator

Bob Ostrom has been illustrating children's books for nearly twenty years. A graduate of the New England School of Art & Design at Suffolk University, Bob has worked for such companies as Disney, Nickelodeon, and Cartoon Network. He lives in North Carolina with his wife Melissa and three children, Will, Charlie, and Mae.